Walt Disney

Jungle Book

Edited by Stella Croker

Longmeadow Press

Hello everybody! Would you like to hear a beautiful story? Here is the adventure of Mowgli, the baby boy who grew up in the jungle. You'll become acquainted with his friends: the wolf family who took good care of him when he was a tiny little baby; Bagheera, the black panther who was wise and experienced; Baloo, the bear who had a very good heart, but didn't think much; all the elephants; and the monkeys and their king, whom one shouldn't trust. Then you will meet with Kaa, the python, who hypnotizes his victims and last of all Shere Khan, the tiger, who is always hungry for man. What is going to happen to little Mowgli amid so many dangers?

That's what you'll find out if you turn the page...

One day, deep in the jungle, as Bagheera was walking he heard a strange noise. It was the sound of someone crying. He looked in the tall grass and there was a baby boy who had been abandoned. Bagheera picked up the baby, but was very puzzled about what to do with him.

Then Bagheera remembered a wolf family that he knew. Akela the father went hunting and mother wolf watched her cubs playing. One more couldn't make that much difference to her. She would certainly agree to adopt this one, he thought.

The little wolf cubs sniffed and sniffed at the little stranger, saying, "What kind of cub is this? We'll call him Mowgli." The baby boy wasn't crying any more and when mother wolf came closer and sniffed him, he smiled. That's how Mowgli found a mother and brothers and sisters.

Mowgli was very happy to live with the wolf family. He and the wolf cubs grew together, playing the same games and having a lot of fun. For ten years, Mowgli lived with the wolves and learned to do everything the wolf cubs could do. He learned to walk; he learned to scratch; he also learned to lie down with his arms and legs up in the air.

On Mowgli's tenth birthday, Bagheera came to visit. He would have liked to have brought a present, but instead he was bringing bad news. Shere Khan, the tiger, had heard about Mowgli and had announced to everyone that the little boy would be his most delicious dessert one of these days. Shere Khan hated all men because one day a hunter had shot at him and ever since then he had wanted revenge. The tiger had decided that as soon as Mowgli was alone, he would kill him so he could not grow up to be a hunter.

A solution had to be found quickly.

When Akela came back from the hunt, the wolves all met on Big Rock. The moon was out and they could see almost as well as in broad daylight. Bagheera repeated what he had heard saying, "I know this sounds very alarming, but there are grounds for my fears. Shere Khan is after Mowgli and will get him unless we act quickly. I am very sad to say that Mowgli must leave at once. He isn't safe here anymore."

"Where will he go?" one of the wolves asked.

"I will take him back to where he belongs: to the man's village. That is the only place where he will be safe." Bagheera had hardly finished saying this when everybody began to argue. But then after a while, they all had to agree that it was the only wise thing to do. The wolves were very sad to let Mowgli go away because they loved him dearly as one of themselves, but there was no time to waste.

When Bagheera went to Mowgli to explain that they
had to leave, Mowgli said "No, I won't go, I want to
stay here with my mother and father. I don't see why I
should go to a village. I want to stay in the jungle, this
is my home." Bagheera told him that he was quite right
to want to stay with the wolves and to love them as
he did, but since Shere Khan was around everything had
changed and it was out of the question for him to stay.

Mowgli jumped up into a tree and was holding on to
the trunk, but Bagheera managed to pull the struggling
and unhappy boy down and, finally, both of them said
good bye to the wolves and then parted from them.
That night, the wolves stayed awake, but they didn't go
hunting because they were much too sad.

Bagheera carried Mowgli away. He didn't stop running for a long time. Mowgli who was usually very talkative didn't speak at all.

"Are you sulking, Mowgli?" Bagheera asked.

"No, not sulking, I'm just thinking," Mowgli replied, "and I'm not scared of Shere Khan."

"Perhaps you aren't," answered Bagheera, "but you should be, because he won't be afraid of you unless you have a gun."

Night was falling, it was
getting darker and darker
and Bagheera stopped in
front of a big tree. He helped
Mowgli get up onto a big
branch. Mowgli who was
very tired didn't argue, but
just snuggled up against
Bagheera and soon they were
both fast asleep.

15

But they weren't alone. Kaa, the snake, was hiding in the tree. Kaa pushed his head down through the leaves. "Is that a boy cub that I see?" hissed Kaa. Bagheera was still sleeping and when Mowgli awoke the first thing he saw was two round eyes staring at him through the leaves. Although Mowgli had never seen Kaa he remembered Akela's warning about the snake. He sat up. "Go away, snake!" shouted Mowgli, staring back at the snake.

That's just what he
shouldn't have done. "I .
don't trust you" he said,
beginning to get dizzy. "You
can trust me," said Kaa. "I
am your friend." He
continued to stare right into
Mowgli's eyes and Mowgli
couldn't look away. He was
under Kaa's spell.

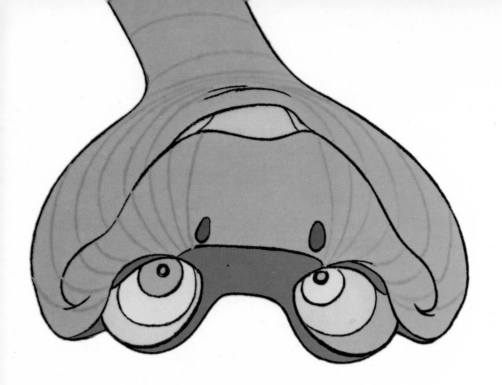

Kaa wrapped his long tail around Mowgli. Still Mowgli couldn't take his eyes off Kaa. Now he was helpless and couldn't move any more. He was Kaa's prey.

"Now I have you! What a good supper!" said Kaa opening his big jaws ready to devour Mowgli. Just at that moment Bagheera, who had heard the noise woke up. He slapped Kaa in the jaw forcing him to free Mowgli. When Bagheera slapped Kaa, there was a big whack, and Kaa fell right down to the ground and landed with a thud. Kaa wiggled away, muttering to himself.

"I hope this will teach you a lesson," grumbled
Bagheera "Kaa tried to get you, Shere Khan the tiger
wants to kill you, too. You are not safe in the jungle
any more, so you must go and live in the man's
village." Mowgli still thought he would rather stay in the
jungle, but didn't say anything because he was a little
upset about what had happened with the snake.

The following day Mowgli again woke up before
Bagheera. He had forgotten about Kaa and Shere Khan;
the sun was bright and Mowgli felt like having fun
on his own. He climbed down from the tree where
Bagheera was still sleeping and ran off. Suddenly Mowgli
heard a loud thumping noise. He climbed up onto a
branch and, just at that moment, saw a troop of
elephants marching along.

Leading the way was Hathi, who was very big and imposing. Several elephants followed and they all marched together under Hathi's command, trumpeting a military march.

Mowgli felt very small next to the big animals, but he liked them anyway, although Hathi, the leader, was very pompous. The whole troop stamped along the path, then at the very end of the line came a very small elephant.

"Hello!" Mowgli said. "Are you going to war?" "Oh no, we're just doing our military routine," answered the baby elephant. "Why don't you join in?"

Mowgli agreed and he immediately joined the troop.

"What a shame mother wolf can't see me!" he thought enjoying pretending to be a soldier.

He marched on, stopped, turned and changed direction, all at Hathi's command.

Even with the wolf cubs he thought he had never had such fun.

Mowgli certainly couldn't compete with the elephants as far as weight was concerned, but he was much more agile and was pretty sure he made a very good soldier.

He and the baby elephant had a marvellous time following Hathi's orders. Once, as Hathi was giving out his orders faster and faster, they bumped into each other and burst into laughter.

They weren't the only ones to become confused, as
Hathi was issuing orders so fast that the elephants
couldn't tell trunks from legs. It was a real tangle by the
time Hathi stopped yelling his orders.

The elephants were tumbling around all heaped up on
top of each other when Hathi shouted "What kind of
soldiers are you? Back to your places! Line up!" but
nobody was listening any more.

It took quite some time before the elephants were able to disentangle themselves. "He shouldn't have yelled out so many orders so fast," Mowgli whispered in the baby elephant's ear.

"Hathi is a big general," answered the small elephant. "He knows his troop very well and you'll see how imposing he is when he inspects us."

"First of all, why should he inspect us?" Mowgli asked, "I don't like being inspected. We should be able to do whatever we want."

The baby elephant didn't really understand what Mowgli meant and just said "Well, we had great fun at any rate!"

All the elephants lined up one after the other. All their trunks were pointed straight up to the sky like trumpets, except no sound was heard. The baby elephant told Mowgli to join in. Both of them stood in line and the baby elephant lifted his trunk too, but couldn't reach any higher than Mowgli's head. Mowgli stood very straight although he was embarrassed by not having a trunk. He stopped breathing to look taller, but wasn't able to hold his breath very long. "Is it going to last very long?" he asked, "I'm getting tired and my muscles are getting stiff."

When Hathi got to Mowgli, he lifted him up with his trunk to have a closer look at this strange animal. "Who are you?" asked Hathi.

"I am a boy, General," Mowgli answered timidly.

"And what, may I ask, are you doing here?" Hathi asked angrily.

Mowgli was beginning to think he should have stayed with Bagheera instead of going off on his own. "Well, Sir, I was playing soldier with the baby elephant," Mowgli answered.

Just then Bagheera, who had been looking for Mowgli, appeared and tried to explain the situation saying, "You'll have to excuse him, General, Mowgli is stubborn. He doesn't mean any harm, but he just doesn't listen. I'm taking him back to the man village," added Bagheera.

Thanks to Bagheera, Hathi calmed down and the two continued on their way. "You're lucky I got there in time, you naughty boy!" Bagheera scolded.

"I would have managed, I can take care of myself!" Mowgli replied.

"That's what you think," snorted Bagheera, "but there are a lot of things you don't know. You do have friends in the jungle, but you also have many enemies and, believe me, they are much stronger than you are," Bagheera went on.

"Oh you're boring," said Mowgli walking away thinking "If only I could find somebody to play with!"

Just then Mowgli heard somebody singing: "Dooby dooby doo, dooby dooby dee, the life of a bear is for me." It was Baloo, a big, happy, singing bear. Mowgli and Baloo soon became friends. "I'll teach you to growl like a bear" said Baloo. And so Mowgli learned to growl.

Then he learned to walk like a bear. He even learned
to fight like a bear. "How am I doing?" asked Mowgli.
"You'd make a great bear!" said Baloo.

Mowgli climbed up onto Baloo's back, saying "I like
travelling with you much better than with Bagheera. He
always tells me what to do and what not to do."

"I think he probably tells you what you must do because he's afraid you'll get into trouble," answered the bear.

"I know," said Mowgli, "he thinks that as soon as I'm away from him I get into all sorts of trouble and that's not true. I just have great fun."

"I'm getting really hungry," said Baloo. "What about you?"

"I'm hungry too. What is there to eat?" asked Mowgli.

"Bananas and honey," came the reply. Mowgli loved
bananas, so both of them started eating, each looking
for the biggest banana to give to the other.

After a while Mowgli said "I think I ate too much, my
stomach is too full."

"I know a very good medicine," Baloo said and he started dancing. Mowgli laughed and joined in the dance. They turned, jumped and spun around.

"That was fun, I feel much better now," giggled Mowgli.

They sat down together to get their breath back. A few minutes later Baloo asked "What about a boxing match?"

"Great! Bagheera always said I'm a light-weight," Mowgli demonstrated by punching Baloo with his fists.

Baloo hardly felt anything, but he pretended to be hurt. "You win," he said. Mowgli was rather pleased with himself.

"I'm very strong." said Mowgli proudly "Bagheera talks a lot of nonsense. I can defend myself very well!"

"Will you tell me a story, Baloo?" Mowgli asked, climbing up to sit on Baloo's shoulders.

They were continuing along the path when Bagheera suddenly popped out of the bushes, saying "Mowgli you are not being very sensible. Shere Khan is nearby looking for you and here you are playing and not worrying about anything. You must come with me now to the man village."

"I want to stay in the jungle," answered Mowgli.
"Baloo will take care of me, won't you Baloo?" he
asked, holding on to Baloo.

"That's right. You can trust me to take good care of
you," said Baloo proudly.

"Will you please let go of my tail. I don't care, do
as you please," snapped Bagheera angrily, "when you see
Shere Khan, you may be sorry you've been so
stubborn."

With that, the black panther disappeared and Baloo
and Mowgli went down to the river.

Up in the trees along the bank of the river the
monkeys were chattering, but Mowgli and Baloo didn't
notice them. Baloo had started singing his song again:
"Dooby dooby doo, dooby dooby dee, the life of a bear
is the life for me."

"It's so good to be in the jungle. Bagheera worries for
no reason at all," Mowgli remarked.

He had hardly finished the sentence when he felt two long and hairy arms grab him and there he was, dangling by the feet. The monkeys wanted to play with him, so they swung Mowgli from tree to tree. They were having such a lot of fun. "Put me down!" cried Mowgli. But the monkeys just laughed some more. Baloo had fallen asleep but, he finally woke up after Mowgli had yelled for help a few times.

"Leave him alone!"
shouted Baloo. "Hee hee
hee" the monkeys sniggered,
"why don't you come and
get him?" And they dangled
Mowgli down right in front
of Baloo.

Baloo got out of the water and started running along under the trees where the monkeys were playing, throwing Mowgli around like a ball. "Monkey faces, will you stop! If I get you, you'll be sorry!" Baloo threatened, but the monkeys couldn't have cared less. Two of them took a vine and held it up in front of Baloo who, being short-sighted, didn't see it and tripped over with a big thud.

Next, all the monkeys disappeared taking Mowgli with them and when Baloo got up and shouted for Mowgli, not a sound was to be heard. "My goodness, where have they taken him?" said Baloo anxiously.

"It's high time that you should worry a little, featherbrain!" said Bagheera. Fortunately he had stayed nearby, anticipating trouble. "I'm sure they have taken Mowgli to their king in the old ruined city. We must go there at once. Follow me and don't make too much noise!" he continued.

Bagheera was right, the monkeys had taken Mowgli to their king and they swung him down out of the trees. "King Louis!" they cried. "Look what we've found."

King Louis scratched his head and said: "He looks a little like a monkey."

"I'm a boy cub!" said Mowgli. Louis picked Mowgli up and swung him around. Mowgli began to feel a little dizzy.

"Let's have a party," said the monkeys.

Bagheera was hiding in the bushes watching for the
best time to jump out and snatch Mowgli away.

When everybody started dancing, a big monkey joined
the party. The big monkey was really Baloo dressed up
as a monkey. He had disguised himself with the help
of a coconut and the monkeys didn't recognize him, but
Mowgli did. Baloo started dancing and all the monkeys
followed him clapping their hands.

King Louis was having a wonderful time. He clapped
in rhythm, faster and faster. Suddenly, Baloo's coconut
fell off and the monkeys recognized him. "The bear, the
bear!" they all shouted.

Baloo grabbed Mowgli. The king did the same and they were both pulling the poor boy, who thought he would be torn apart.

Suddenly one of the columns which the king was holding on to began crumbling away and there was a big noise as if the whole temple was about to collapse.

The king dropped Mowgli and rushed over to hold up
the temple. Baloo who liked to imitate stood in place of
another column saying "How strong we are! We carry a
whole palace on our backs!"

Then an idea crossed Baloo's mind and he rushed over to tickle King Louis. "It's not easy to hold a palace on your shoulders when someone is tickling you, is it?" he asked. "You're making wonderful faces, it's even better than going to the circus!".

"Baloo, Baloo, help!" Hearing Mowgli shouting for help was enough for Baloo to forget about his pranks. He stopped tickling King Louis and ran over to where Bagheera had just found Mowgli.

It was more than time for them to escape because the whole palace began to collapse around them.

When the three friends reached safety, they sat down
together. Bagheera said "You see where all this has led
to. You're very lucky that I'm always there to keep an
eye on you. Now we really have to go to the man
village. That's where you belong."

"No, I won't live in the man village. I want to stay in
the jungle!" Mowgli shouted and he ran away into the
jungle.

He liked walking in the tall grass. "If they try to make me leave the jungle," he thought, "I'll stay by myself, or I'll go back to mother wolf." Suddenly he heard a long hissing sound and, looking down, he saw Kaa the snake slithering towards him out of the grass.

"Hello Mowgli" Kaa said, "happy to see you again."

"You're a liar" retorted Mowgli "and besides I'm not looking into your eyes again because I know your tricks now!" But it was too late, the snake was already hypnotizing him.

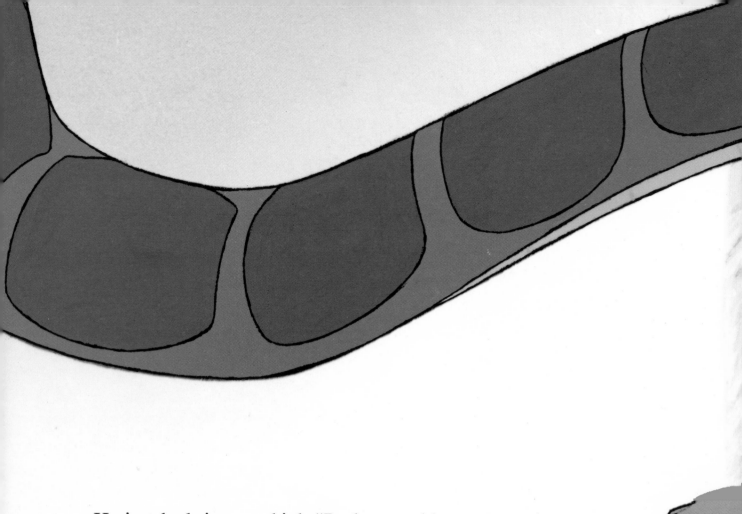

He just had time to think "Bagheera told me to watch out for the snake." And then he couldn't think any more; he was getting dizzier and dizzier as if he was falling asleep with his eyes wide open. Kaa was hissing and beginning to coil up around Mowgli.

"This time, you won't run away from me. Shere Khan thought he was going to be the one who ate you. He is stronger, but I'm more cunning!" the snake said.

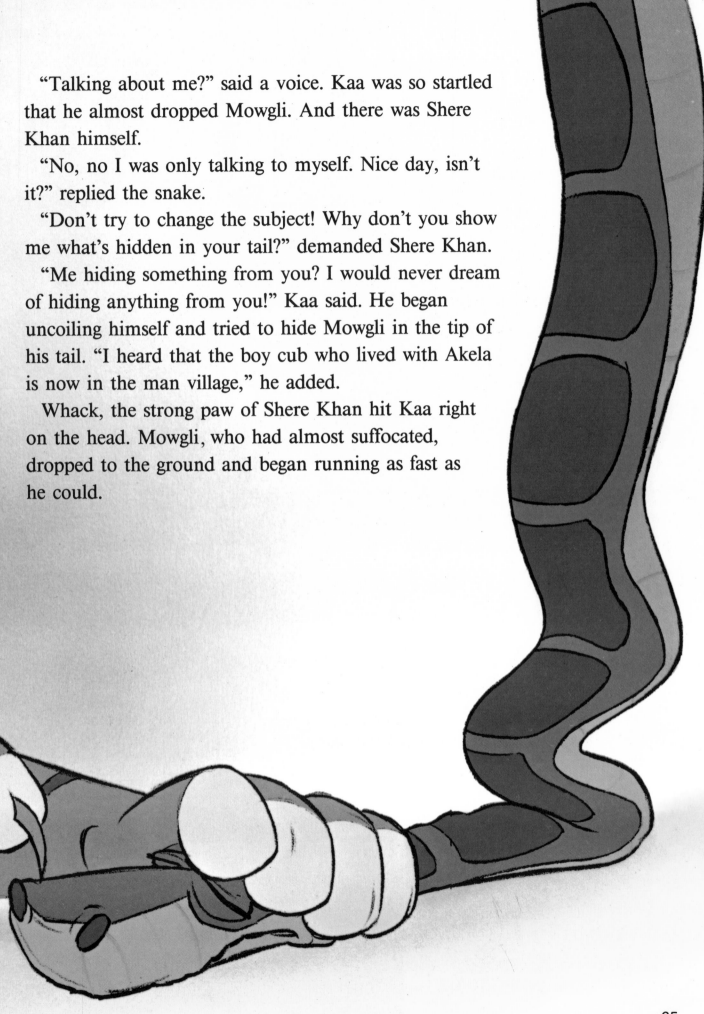

"Talking about me?" said a voice. Kaa was so startled that he almost dropped Mowgli. And there was Shere Khan himself.

"No, no I was only talking to myself. Nice day, isn't it?" replied the snake.

"Don't try to change the subject! Why don't you show me what's hidden in your tail?" demanded Shere Khan.

"Me hiding something from you? I would never dream of hiding anything from you!" Kaa said. He began uncoiling himself and tried to hide Mowgli in the tip of his tail. "I heard that the boy cub who lived with Akela is now in the man village," he added.

Whack, the strong paw of Shere Khan hit Kaa right on the head. Mowgli, who had almost suffocated, dropped to the ground and began running as fast as he could.

Mowgli ran as long as he
could in the direction away
from Shere Khan. Then the
jungle suddenly seemed very
dark. Mowgli saw wings
fluttering and lots of long
beaks as a flight of vultures
landed just in front of him.
Mowgli sat very still on a
rock, wondering what was
going to happen to him next.
He'd heard bad things about
vultures. For the moment
they didn't look as if they
meant any harm to him.
"Hello Mowgli, pleased to
meet you," one of the
vultures said. "We saw you
several times when you were
with Akela."

"We would like to be your friends," another one said. "Wouldn't you like to play with us?" a third one continued. Mowgli hesitated because he remembered that vultures were usually not considered to be trustworthy, but as he looked at them he thought that probably Bagheera and the wolves would have found these particular vultures rather friendly.

"All right, let's play!" Mowgli finally said, "But I don't know how to fly."

"We'll teach you!" said the vultures beginning to push and pull and to turn Mowgli around. Mowgli jumped in the air and tried to flutter his arms, but he always fell back onto the ground.

"I always fall down," he said.

The vultures encouraged him saying, "Keep trying. You'll get better and better and you'll certainly end up by flying."

While Mowgli was making unsuccessful attempts to fly, Shere Khan had followed his tracks and was observing the scene, thinking to himself "Stupid boy cub who thinks he is a bird!" and he leapt out of the bushes with a big roar.

All the vultures flew away and Mowgli was left alone with the tiger. "This time, you can't get away from me!" snarled Shere Khan.

Mowgli was very scared, but he tried not to show it. So here he was with his worst enemy and no one to help him! He was forgetful, but not a coward so he gathered up his courage and said: "I am not afraid of you."

"You must be afraid of me," said Shere Khan. "Everyone is afraid of me."

"Well, I'm not!" said Mowgli. "Look!" said the tiger. "I will count to ten. You must try to get away."

Shere Khan began to count. "One, two, three, four..."

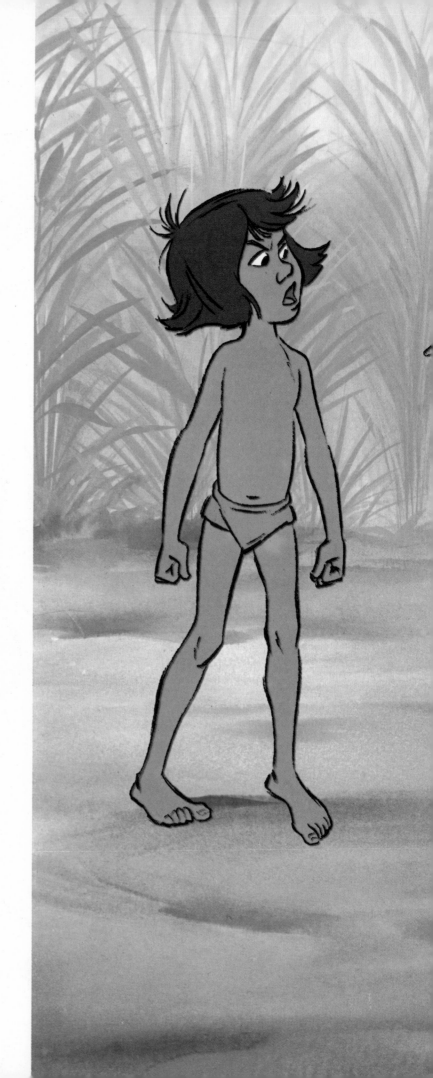

"Get ready, Mowgli!" shouted one vulture.

"Run, run, quickly!" said another. But Mowgli knew that Shere Khan could run so fast that if he tried to escape, he would very soon be caught.

Instead, he grabbed a branch and decided that he would fight even if he didn't stand much chance with the tiger. The tiger, furious to see the little boy stand up to him, gave a loud roar and showed his big claws.

The tiger crouched ready to pounce. But, just as he was ready to leap, he was stopped by Baloo, who was hiding behind a tree. He jumped out in front of the tiger and held his big paw over Shere Khan's, shouting: "Leave the boy cub alone!"

"Move out of the way. We'll see who gives orders in the forest," the big tiger proudly said. "I am the King of the forest."

Baloo grabbed Shere Khan's tail and held on so that he couldn't move. "Run, Mowgli, run!" Baloo yelled. Mowgli started running and he could still feel Shere Khan's hot breath on his neck. The sky was very dark now and black clouds were mounting up over the jungle.

Suddenly there was a big flash of lightning and a loud
clap of thunder. Mowgli had the feeling he wasn't being
followed any more. He climbed up on a tree and tried
to catch his breath.

The thunder was getting louder and louder and the lightning was very bright, but most of the time it was as dark as a pit. Mowgli had imagined he was safe much too soon. Shere Khan had found him once more and was circling around the tree on which Mowgli was perched. "I am trapped!" Mowgli thought. "He'll stay by the tree until I fall down and then he'll eat me!" He felt like crying, but after all, this situation was his own fault. If only he had listened to Bagheera!

Just then a big flash of lightning appeared in the sky. It crashed through the trees and Shere Khan let out a terrible roar. Mowgli's tree had caught on fire. The vultures somehow lifted Mowgli to safety and put him down on the ground. Mowgli immediately saw that Shere Khan was scared of the fire, so he picked up a burning branch and held it out in front of himself.

Mowgli had found a weapon that would save his life
if he was smart enough. Mowgli thought of his friends
Bagheera and Baloo and he felt brave again.

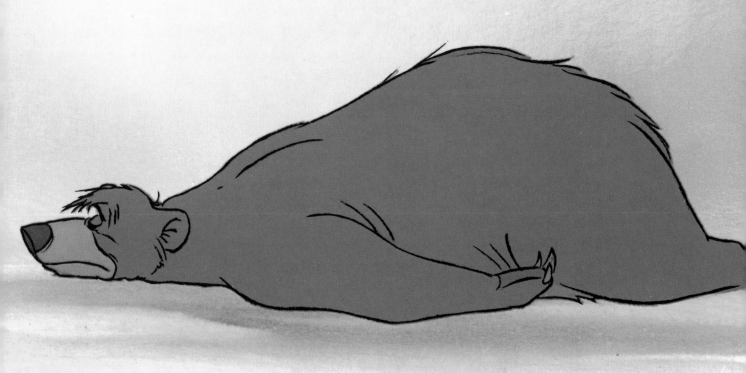

Shere Khan was watching Mowgli and slowly approaching the boy, his eyes burning with greed.

"This time, boy cub, you won't be able to escape!" Shere Khan said. The vultures who had waited to help Mowgli swooped down on the tiger and pecked him with their beaks. "Fly away, stupid animals! I'll tear you to pieces!" roared Shere Khan.

Meanwhile Mowgli had an opportunity to carry out his plan. He tied the burning branch to Shere Khan's tail. The tiger screamed with pain and he raced away into the forest.

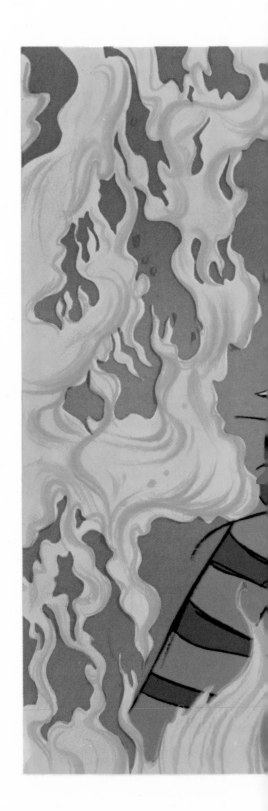

Mowgli sighed with relief. He was even happier when he saw Baloo and Bagheera reappear. He told them what had happened and they were both very proud of Mowgli. All three were very tired, so they looked for a place to recover from the day's adventures. As soon as they had found one, they all fell soundly asleep.

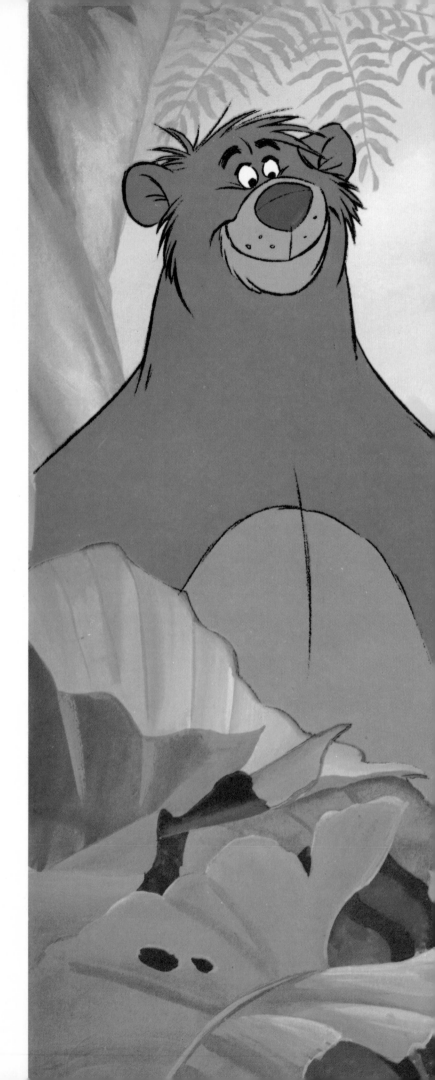

The following morning,
Mowgli was forced to admit
that life in the jungle was
quite dangerous for a boy
and he was willing to go to
the man village. So the three
friends started off towards
the village. Bagheera and
Baloo were a little worried as
to how Mowgli would
manage once they got there.

When they got close to the
village, they saw a river.

They heard someone singing. They crept closer and, just behind the branches, was a young girl getting some water. "This is a girl cub," Bagheera informed the others. "She looks a lot like me," agreed Mowgli.

"Maybe I will live here for a while." He had never seen such a nice creature. Mowgli looked at Bagheera enquiringly.

"Go ahead, Mowgli!" said the wise black panther.

Although he was still
scared Mowgli moved a little
closer. Up until now he had
never seen human creatures.
He thought of the wolves, of
Bagheera and of his life in
the jungle. He also
remembered that he had said
the jungle was where he
belonged, but for the first
time in his life he knew he,
too, was a human being.

He looked again at his friends and smiled at them. Then he turned back and saw the young girl's face reflected in the water. When he stepped forward she heard the noise and turned towards him. She wasn't afraid when she saw him. In fact she smiled at him and asked him: "What is your name? I've never seen you before."

"My name is Mowgli," he answered. The girl was lifting her water jug and Mowgli offered to help. Mowgli carried the water jug and they walked together to the village, the girl showing Mowgli the way. From time to time, she stopped and smiled at him.

"I think Mowgli will stay in the man village," said Bagheera.

"Yes," agreed Baloo. "but I think he would have made a great bear anyway." The two friends went back together to the jungle where they belonged and that is where Mowgli's story ends.

This edition produced exclusively for
Longmeadow Press
by Twin Books

ISBN 0-681-40106-0

Printed in Hong Kong